D1156904

MONSTER
HUNTERS
Spot the Loveland Frog

by Jan Fields
Illustrated by Scott Brundage

Calico

An Imprint of Magic Wagon
abdobooks.com

abdobooks.com

Published by Magic Wagon, a division of ABDO, PO Box 398166, Minneapolis, Minnesota 55439. Copyright © 2019 by Abdo Consulting Group, Inc. International copyrights reserved in all countries. No part of this book may be reproduced in any form without written permission from the publisher. Calico™ is a trademark and logo of Magic Wagon.

Printed in the United States of America, North Mankato, Minnesota.
102018
012019

 THIS BOOK CONTAINS
RECYCLED MATERIALS

Written by Jan Fields
Illustrated by Scott Brundage
Edited by Tamara L. Britton
Design Contributors: Candice Keimig & Laura Mitchell

Library of Congress Control Number: 2018947945

Publisher's Cataloging-in-Publication Data

Names: Fields, Jan, author. | Brundage, Scott, illustrator.
Title: Spot the Loveland frog / by Jan Fields; illustrated by Scott Brundage.
Description: Minneapolis, Minnesota : Magic Wagon, 2019. | Series: Monster
    hunters set 3
Summary: The Monster Hunters head to Ohio to investigate the Loveland
    Frog for their Discover Cryptids Internet show. Ben's friend George is
    making a film about the creature. George's three sisters are wearing
    frogman suits in the film. But why are there four frogmen in one scene?
Identifiers: ISBN 9781532133695 (lib. bdg.) | ISBN 9781532134296 (ebook) |
ISBN 9781532134593 (Read-to-me ebook)
Subjects: LCSH: Monsters--Juvenile fiction. | Movie-making--Juvenile
    fiction. | Internet videos--Juvenile fiction.
Classification: DDC [FIC]--dc23

TABLE of CONTENTS

chapter 1

BEAST
OF BUSCO

On a hot day in Churubusco, Indiana, Gabe, Tyler, and Sean stood in the line for the helicopter ride. Gabe yelped when the man in front of him stepped backwards and trod on his sneaker. The man looked down at him. "Sorry kid. You need to be more careful."

"Me?" Gabe yelped, but the man had already turned around. He and his wife ran to the helicopter for their ride.

"We're next!" Tyler yelled in Gabe's ear.

Gabe winced at his best friend's loud voice, but nodded. None of them had ever ridden in a helicopter. They were all excited, even though Sean kept calling out terrifying helicopter accident facts.

Gabe carried one of the team's smaller cameras. His older brother Ben had sent them to shoot some footage to use as B-roll for their Internet show, *Discover Cryptids*. The show examined creatures from myth or legend that might be real, or might have been real at one time.

Gabe loved shooting the extra footage that could be edited into the show when needed. B-roll gave viewers something interesting to look at whenever Ben's voice-over explained something.

Tyler yelled in Gabe's ear again, "After we're done, we can get some fried dough."

Gabe laughed. Tyler was always thinking about his stomach. Luckily, the Churubusco Turtle Days Festival had plenty of great things to eat. Though no one had seen the giant turtle in years, the small Indiana town was certainly proud of it. The team was there so Ben could do an episode about how cryptids often became tourist attractions.

Ben planned to do a whole season of episodes about how cryptid legends affect people. Gabe wasn't sure that was a good idea. He would rather look for the creatures themselves, but Ben was the boss.

Sean stared down at his computer tablet. "According to this site," he announced, "a helicopter is thirty-five percent more likely to crash than an airplane."

"You're bringing down the mood here," Tyler told him.

Sean looked up at Tyler. "Why?"

"We're getting ready to get in a helicopter," Gabe explained. "We don't want to think about crashing."

"That's illogical," Sean said. "This is the time we need crash information the most."

To Gabe's relief, it was their turn to ride so he

didn't need to answer Sean. They hurried out to the helicopter. Sean and Tyler scrambled into the back seats of the small helicopter. Gabe sat in the front where he could get a better view for shooting video.

As soon as they got their headphones on, Sean began rattling off questions about the helicopter's safety checks. The pilot answered patiently as they lifted off and flew over the festival.

Then Sean launched into a bunch of statistics about helicopter accidents. "Most accidents are caused by pilot error," Sean said. "So you need to be careful."

"I'm always careful," the pilot said. Gabe could hear the annoyance in the man's voice.

"Sean," Gabe spoke up. "Maybe you should just look at the scenery."

"Hey, look at that," Tyler shouted into the microphone. "Guys, look at that. It's the turtle!"

As he shouted, Tyler hopped up and down in his seat as much as the seat belts would let him.

"Just calm down, kid," the pilot insisted.

"Calm down!" Tyler yelled back. "It's the turtle. Look, Sean, film it!"

Gabe looked out the front window, but he didn't see anything unusual. They were passing over a narrow road that was partially obscured by woods. "I don't see anything."

"It's under the trees," Tyler was still yelling. "Turn around! It's under the trees."

"Stop yelling," the pilot said, his own voice loud in Gabe's ears.

"Get closer!" Tyler yelled.

"No," Sean insisted. "Stay away from the trees. Tree strikes have caused fatal helicopter accidents on more than one occasion. I'll find the exact number." His voice trailed off.

"I don't need the exact number," the pilot shouted. "And I'm not going to hit a tree. What I do need is for you kids to calm down."

"There!" Tyler yelled, his voice even louder. "I saw it through the trees for a second."

"Stop that!" the pilot yelled.

Gabe twisted in his seat to see. Tyler was practically pressed against the side of the helicopter, trying to see behind them.

"That's it!" the pilot shouted. He raced ahead above the road.

"Not so fast," Tyler yelled, bouncing in his seat again. "It's back there."

The pilot finally set the copter down in a clearing. "Listen up. Your behavior is putting us in danger."

"You seem to be emotionally upset," Sean said. "I could find the statistics on the number of helicopter accidents linked to emotional upset in the pilot."

"No more!" the pilot roared. "No more statistics. No more imaginary turtles. You boys behave, or I'm putting you out right here and you can call your parents to come get you."

"That would be difficult," Sean said calmly. "My parents are several states away."

Gabe groaned as the pilot's face turned a shade of red that Gabe associated with fire trucks, not calm adults. Then before the pilot could throw them off the helicopter, Tyler screamed, pointing out the front windscreen of the helicopter.

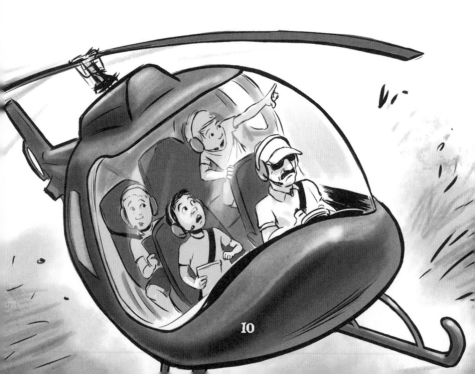

Gabe turned and added his own yells. A giant turtle burst from the tree line. It was nearly as big as the whole helicopter. It raced at them fast, its huge jaws snapping.

chapter 2

THE FROGMEN ARE HERE

"I wasn't scared," Tyler said. He sat slumped in the van seat, his arms crossed.

"Are you still sulking?" Ben asked, glancing back at the boys in the rearview mirror.

"Tyler has been sulking for three hours and twenty-six minutes," Sean said. "Or two hundred and two miles. Approximately."

"You know," Tyler said. "Your love for numbers is kind of irritating."

"At least I wasn't afraid of a parade float."

"It was scary," Gabe said. "And none of us knew it was a parade float until it went by."

"I determined it was a manufactured turtle immediately," Sean said.

Of course you did. Gabe sighed deeply and

looked out the window at the neighborhoods of Loveland, Ohio. The houses were mostly small and neat. The lawns were trimmed. In one front yard, a little boy played ball with his dog. Both stopped to stare at the van as it passed.

"Have you noticed people stare at us?" Gabe called to his brother.

Ben met his gaze in the rearview mirror. "Good. The van wrap is working!"

"Yeah." Gabe sighed. It was working to make them look silly. Like Tyler, he'd felt a little foolish after the turtle, and now this.

Right after they reached a million subscribers for the show, Ben had the van covered in thin vinyl decals. *Discover Cryptids* ran down both sides with creatures peering out from behind the lettering. The decals also gave the web address for their Internet show.

"Are we going to eat soon?" Tyler yelled from the seat ahead of Gabe.

"We're meeting George at a convenience store so you can probably go in and get a hot dog," Ben suggested. "We're almost there."

"Excellent!" Tyler bounced in his seat.

"Hot dogs are made from scrap meats of questionable origin," Sean said. He sat behind Gabe. As usual, Sean rarely spoke unless he had some new fact to share. Of course, he always had some new fact to share. Sometimes the facts were interesting. Sometimes, not so much.

"Don't tell me about it!" Tyler shouted. He clamped his hands over his ears. "Do not ruin hot dogs for me."

Sean didn't even raise his voice. "I am not responsible for your feelings about hot dogs." He paused, then added, "And the most effective method of blocking sound with your hand is to stick your fingers in your ears."

"Thanks for the tip!" Tyler said, sticking his fingers in his ears.

Gabe sighed again. When Sean and Tyler started arguing, it was definitely time to get out of the van. He spoke loudly to be heard over the hot dog discussion. "Will your friend be at the store when we get there?"

"You never know with George. If he got caught up with filming this afternoon, he could be late," Ben said.

Finally, they pulled in at the convenience store. The lot was mostly empty except for one old, banged-up car. "Not here," Gabe said.

"Sure he is," his brother answered. "That's George's car right there. It's a classic."

Tyler scooted across his seat to press his nose against the window. "Where? All I see is that rust bucket."

"That's the one," Ben said. "It will be a beauty when he's done restoring it."

"You mean he's started?" Tyler asked.

"Listen, you guys," Ben said as he pulled into

a parking space. "No one make fun of George's car. He loves that thing."

Gabe grabbed his camera as they piled out of the van. He knew there wasn't likely to be anything to film here, but he tried always to be prepared. The door opened and a short, muscular guy with a huge grin rushed out. "B-man!" he yelled.

"Georginator!" Ben yelled back.

Tyler made a quiet gagging noise near Gabe.

Ben and George went through a long series of fist bump, hand shake, finger wiggling gestures that ended in a hug. It was easily the weirdest thing Gabe had ever seen his brother do.

"George," Ben said, his voice still overloud. "You haven't met my baby brother."

Gabe frowned. Baby?

George stomped over and hugged Gabe, lifting him clear off the ground and making his ribs creak. Finally, he set Gabe down and yelled

in his face. "Glad to meet you, little dude!"

"Do you have hearing problems?" Sean asked, genuine curiosity on his face.

George looked at him for a moment, then burst out laughing before shouting back at Ben. "I like this kid. He's funny!"

"Sean is part of my team for the show," Ben said, his own volume turned down considerably. Obviously, he'd known Sean wasn't kidding. He swept a hand toward Tyler who was running toward the store, probably going for a hot dog. "And there goes the last member of my team. His name is Tyler."

"That kid can run," George boomed. "I don't know where my people have run off to." He shrugged. "They'll be back in a minute, I'm sure."

"Ben said you're doing a movie about the Loveland Frog," Gabe said.

George bobbed his head. "I'm writing a kind

of horror movie, but in my story, it's the people who are bad. The frogmen are the heroes."

"In 1972, several frogman reports were actually based on an escaped iguana," Sean said. "The animal was eventually shot by a police officer."

George crossed his arms over his chest. "Maybe, but that doesn't explain the man in 1955 who saw three frogmen. Nor does it explain the couple that took pictures of a frogman in 2016."

Ben clapped his hands. "Let's not debate now. We're hoping to get some footage of your movie in the making. When are you filming next?"

"Shortly, I just have to collect the rest of my crew." He looked around and frowned. "They're here somewhere. They said something about getting a snack."

As the rest of the group headed for the store, Gabe didn't follow. He lifted the camera and panned the brush at the edge of the parking lot. He didn't expect to shoot any decent footage, but with the sun setting, there was an interesting glow to everything.

Then Gabe gasped as his camera focused sharply on a log in the brush. Three frogmen sat hunched over with their backs to him. He could see the three nodding and shifting on the log.

The frogmen were real!

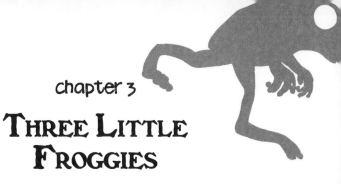

chapter 3

THREE LITTLE FROGGIES

Gabe held the camera up and bellowed for his brother. He worried that his yelling would make the frogmen run away, but instead they stood and turned toward him. Clutched in each flipper was a mostly eaten ice cream on a stick. Ice cream?

He jerked the camera upwards in surprise. It focused on the head of one frogman. The head bobbed and wobbled, eyes staring blankly at the sky. At the sky?

"What are you doing?" one of the frogmen demanded. The voice was high and young. Frog kids?

Gabe lowered his camera and looked at the creatures with his eyes. Then he groaned. The head of each creature bobbed and wobbled because it had been pushed up and off the real heads of the people underneath. The frogmen were kids. In fact, they were girls. Girls with round brown faces that looked almost exactly alike.

"Oh, you found my team," George said from behind him. He pointed at the frog girls. "I told you guys not to wander off."

"We just wanted someplace to sit down," the first girl said. She had her springy black hair done up into two poofs.

"We would have sat on the car," the second girl said. Her hair was braided close to her head. "But you don't like food on your precious rust bucket."

"Hey, don't dis my car," George said. "Now come up here and meet the *Discover Cryptids* crew."

George turned toward Ben. "These three are my sisters." He pointed at each in turn and rattled off their names. The girl with the two poofs was Meg. The girl with the braids was Jo, and the third girl whose hair stood out around her head like black dandelion fluff was Amy.

"We're triplets," Amy said, then she slurped the last of the ice cream from her stick.

Meg rolled her eyes. "Mom was reading *Little Women* before we were born. That's why we have weird names."

"None of us was named Beth," Jo added, "because she dies."

"Spoilers!" Meg and Amy yelled at her.

Jo put her frog hands on her hips. "Oh, like they are going to read *Little Women*."

"They might," Meg said.

George clapped his hands. "Forget the book. We have to get going if we're going to catch the light for our last shoot."

"Oh boy," Amy said. "More slopping around in the mud."

As they walked back to the parking lot, Ben asked, "What are you shooting tonight?"

"The original 1955 sighting," George said. "The frogmen are spotted and then run off."

"Not that we can run much in these feet," Jo complained as she lifted her oversized feet high to avoid tripping in the brush.

"You guys should have stayed on the pavement," George said. "I don't want you tearing those suits."

The girls grumbled as they stomped along.

Gabe was amazed as how much they looked like frogs when they walked. He backed up until he was walking beside Jo. "Do you think there really were frogmen?"

"I don't really care. This movie was supposed to be fun. George promised. But eating ice cream in the weeds is the most fun we've had so far." She licked her ice cream stick one more time, then tucked it into the front of her suit. "You never know when you might need a stick."

Gabe didn't know what to say to that, so they crossed the parking lot with the flapping of her big feet as the only sound. When they reached George's rusty car, Jo turned suddenly to face him. "Something weird did happen last night."

"Weird?"

She bobbed her head. "That's why we have to reshoot. These big glowing eyes showed in the background when George played back the video."

26

Sean must have heard what she said. He stepped away from the van and said, "Many nocturnal animal eyes will glow with reflected light."

"That's what George said too. But these eyes were big. Giant sized. Anything with eyes that big is scary." She shivered. "I don't really want to go back there tonight. My sisters don't either."

"Then why are you?" Gabe asked.

Again, Jo shrugged. "It's George's film. He's the boss. And he's bossy enough to prove it." She reached out and patted Gabe's arm with one flipper hand. "I'm glad you guys will be there. If you see something. Get us out of there. Fast!"

chapter 4

THE FROG'S CURSE

They met the rest of George's crew alongside a country road not far from the gas station.

The scene was simple enough, one of the crew drove George's car down the road in the dark. The three frog girls had to crouch by the side of the road. When the headlights hit them, they would jump up, scramble over the guardrail, and rush into the woods.

Even with a simple scene, the set up took a while. As Gabe and the guys watched, the crew attached a camera to the inside of George's car to shoot from the perspective of the car's driver.

In another place, men were unloading a rig from a van. It looked like a really short bit of railroad track with a big camera. Gabe knew it was for shooting smooth shots with a moving camera. He felt a pang of jealousy at the sight of the fancy equipment. They didn't have nearly such nice stuff for *Discover Cryptids*.

"This time," George yelled as the set up was nearly finished, "I want someone out there with a bullhorn, making a lot of noise just before we shoot. If there's any wildlife in the area, I want it scared off." He pointed at a tall, lanky crewman with a patch of beard on his chin.

The crewman threw George a mock salute. "Aye, aye."

George turned to Ben. "If you guys want to get some shots, that's fine. But make sure the kids stay out of the crew's way."

"My guys are pros," Ben said. "They know to stay clear of your cameras."

"Sure," George said. "Good."

Gabe carried a night vision camera over to the edge of the clearing, out of the way of the crew. He started filming the woods to see if any wildlife might turn up, but mostly he stewed about George. Though glad Ben stood up for them, he still didn't like the things George said.

The slap of flippers behind him made Gabe turn as Jo walked over. "See anything?"

Gabe was glad of the darkness around him as his cheeks warmed. He had barely paid attention. "I won't know for sure until I play it back," he stammered.

"Can I see?"

Gabe turned the viewer toward Jo, it showed the woods around them in shades of green. Mostly the view was splotchy and nothing seemed to be moving. Gabe panned the camera over the woods then he jumped, nearly dropping the camera in his surprise.

Something big was headed through the woods toward them! Whatever it was, it walked upright. Gabe could see the creature picking its legs up high like the girls had in their frog costumes.

"What's that?" Jo squeaked. Her sisters squeezed in close beside her.

"I'm not sure," Gabe answered.

Then a voice called out. "Hey! What are you people doing here?"

Gabe lowered the night vision camera as the crew turned lights toward the sound. They lit up an older man wearing hip waders. The man threw an arm up in front of his face at the bright lights. "You trying to blind me?"

"Sir," George yelled. "We're filming here. I'm going to have to ask you to get out of the camera line."

"Filming." The man blinked and waded the rest of the way toward them. "What are you all filming out here?"

"A horror movie," Meg yelled back at him. She stood near the rail beside Amy.

The man looked at their frog costumes and frowned. "You making fun of the frogman?"

"No," George answered. "I'm just making a movie."

"The frogmen won't like that," the man said.

32

He pointed a bent finger at George. "And you're risking the Loveland curse."

George barked out a laugh. "A curse? That would be awesome."

"I don't want to be cursed," Amy whimpered.

"There is no curse associated with the legend of the Loveland Frog," Sean said. Sean could never let a factually incorrect statement go.

The man looked sharply at Sean. "You from around here, kid?"

"No," Sean said, looking up into the man's scowl without flinching. Gabe knew that when it came to defending truth, Sean was fearless. "Though I have researched Ohio extensively."

"Well, I've lived here all my life, and I'm telling you." He raised his voice and looked around at the group. "I'm telling all of you. If you keep this up, this movie is going to be cursed!"

"I want to go home," Amy wailed. "I want to go home now!"

chapter 5

FLIPPER
FLOP

The man stomped off. George calmed his sisters down. Filming went on, though not without a hitch.

One of the flippers on Meg's suit was torn. As she stepped off the road into the swamp, the cold water hit her foot and she began shrieking. Then two of the cameras simply stopped working, and no one could figure out why. When someone dropped a boom mic into the swampy water, George called a halt to the filming.

"It's the curse," Amy whimpered.

Sean overhead her. "There is no curse connected to the Loveland Frog," he insisted.

The girls didn't answer. They just waddled toward George's car.

George's loud clap made all three boys jump. "Let's get packed up, people! We're going to have an early day tomorrow. And I want all the cameras working by then."

A chorus of half-hearted agreement met the order. Gabe followed George's sisters to find out if it was normal to have so many problems. For all he knew, all movies had problems.

He found the sisters pulling off their frog costumes and tossing them into the trunk of George's car. Meg was still grumbling about her wet foot. "Who knows what kinds of germs swim around in that muck?"

"You should ask Sean," Gabe suggested. "He could probably tell you exactly what germs swim around in swamps."

Meg rolled her eyes at him. "Like I want to know."

"How did you get a hole in your flipper?" he asked.

Meg shrugged. "I don't know. I left them near the railing when I switched to flip-flops."

"You shouldn't have taken them off," Jo scolded.

"I was worn out from walking around that store parking lot," Meg complained. "I needed the break." She reached into the trunk and hauled out a muddy flipper boot. She thrust it at Gabe. "It's a big hole. I don't know how we're going to fix it."

Gabe pulled a small flashlight from his pocket and shone it on the flipper. The hole was obvious.

"Oh no!" Amy shrieked. "Something bit your flipper!"

It did look like something had chewed on the rubber. He held it up to his face to see it better.

"Wow," Amy said. "I wouldn't put that stinky thing so close to my face."

Gabe turned the flipper over and over. "It looks chewed."

"That doesn't make sense," Jo scoffed. "It was right at the railing, and we were all around it. What animal would come chew on a rubber boot with so many people around?"

"A monster," Amy suggested. "A cursed monster."

"I doubt it was a monster." Gabe looked up at Meg. "Do you mind if I take some photos of this?"

"Sure. Knock yourself out."

Gabe pulled out his cellphone and took some photos with it. He handed the boot back to Meg. "Do you guys usually have so many technical problems?"

Amy shook her head. "I figure it's the curse."

"Don't be a goose," Jo snapped. "There's no such thing."

"There might be," Amy said stubbornly. "Lots of movie sets have been cursed."

The triplets launched into a lively argument

about whether curses existed. Gabe tried to ask more questions, but the girls ignored him as they yelled at one another. Finally, Gabe huffed and walked back to the van.

The doors at the back of the van were open, and Tyler stood in the glow of the van light. He was packing up their night vision camera. "Where'd you go?" he asked.

"I was talking to the triplets," he said. "And I saw the flipper. It looked chewed." He showed Tyler the photos he'd taken.

"That's a big bite," Tyler said nervously.

"Could be swamp rats." Sean's face appeared over the back of the last seat. "Rats can be very bold. And they often sample unknown foods to see if they're edible."

"That was a big bite," Tyler insisted. "So, it must have been a really stupid swamp rat."

"There is no such thing as a swamp rat here," Sean said. "The two rats found in Ohio are the Norway rat and the Allegheny Woodrat. The Woodrat is a kind of pack rat, and it's endangered."

"How do you know so much about rats?" Gabe asked.

Sean blinked at him. "I know about almost everything."

Tyler groaned at that, then turned to Gabe. "Maybe the curse made the rat chew on the boot. I really don't like curses."

"Cryptids don't have curses. I've been looking it up." Sean held up his tablet computer to prove it.

Tyler pointed at him. "The Jersey Devil was supposed to be caused by a curse."

Sean wrinkled his nose. "I'm not counting that one. The cryptid isn't cursing anyone in that story. The Rougarou is also supposed to be a cursed creature, but I don't think that's the same situation either."

"The Rougarou?" Gabe said.

"It's a kind of werewolf," Sean said.

"None of that explains why everything went wrong tonight after that old guy cursed the movie," Tyler insisted. "I think we need to get out of here before we get some kind of secondhand cursing."

"You don't have to be scared," Sean insisted. "It's like the turtle float. This isn't real."

Tyler's face darkened and he crossed his arms. "I'm not scared."

"You sound scared," Sean said.

Gabe did not want to listen to more arguing. "Where's Ben?"

"He went to help George pack up," Tyler said and pointed. Gabe turned and saw Ben looking at one of the cameras.

Finally, Ben seemed to be done and walked over to the van. "You guys ready to go?"

Tyler leaned against the back of the van with

his arms crossed, glaring at Sean. "We were waiting on you. And we weren't scared."

"Um, that's good," Ben said. "I wanted to look at the camera that broke down. I don't think it was normal wear and tear."

"That's because it was the curse," Tyler said.

"Actually, I think the camera was tampered with. Which means someone is helping the curse along. Someone is trying to ruin George's movie."

chapter 6

WHAT BIG EYES YOU HAVE

Once they were in their hotel room, Sean immediately opened up his laptop to get on the Internet. Gabe said, "I think you better tell us more about the Loveland Frog."

"And the curse," Tyler added.

"I told you," Sean said, looking up from his computer. "There's no curse."

Gabe sat down on the bed beside Tyler. "Someone is using the legend to create this fake curse. We need to know everything about the legend."

Sean sat up straighter. He loved this part. "According to a local legend, one night in 1955, a businessman saw three frogmen beside the road. He stopped his car for a closer look. He

43

said the frogmen were three or four feet tall."

Tyler sat up then. "About the size of George's sisters."

Sean gave him an annoyed glance for the interruption. "Yes, about that size. The man said they had heads like frogs and webbed hands, but they walked on two feet. We know he saw them somewhere near the bridge and around the Branch Hill community."

"That was a long time ago," Gabe said. "They would be really old frogs today."

"According to a Loveland police officer, the creatures aren't still around," Sean said. "In 1972, he said he shot a large iguana. He said the iguana was the creature people were seeing."

Tyler crossed his arms. "I don't know why someone would shoot an iguana. My cousin has one. They don't hurt anyone."

"At the time, the officer didn't know what the thing was," Sean said.

"He was probably freaked out, especially if he grew up with the original frogman stories," Gabe said.

"The iguana didn't have a tail," Sean added, "but it also didn't stand on two legs, of course. I'm not sure shooting an iguana really disproved the original story. And it certainly doesn't explain this." He turned to his computer and brought up a video.

The image quality wasn't great. Mostly it just showed reflections on dark water with a vague shadowy shape and glowing eyes. "This was filmed with a cell phone in July 2016," Sean said.

"Hey," Tyler said. "Didn't the triplets say they saw big glowing eyes like that on the video they shot?"

"They did," Gabe agreed. "I think we need to look at that. I'll see if Ben can get a copy."

He headed toward the door and Tyler leaped

off the bed to join him. Sean showed no interest in following. "Bring a copy back, so I can analyze it," he said before turning his full attention back to his computer.

When Gabe rapped on Ben's door, there was no answer, not even when Tyler joined in with some aggressive pounding. "He's probably down in George's room," Gabe said, looking down the corridor. He wasn't sure if his brother would welcome him interrupting. But he doubted he could sleep unless he did something to investigate what was going on.

George answered the door quickly and grinned down at Gabe and Tyler before turning to look back into the room. "Ben, your team is here." Gabe flinched at the way George said "team," as if he found the word funny.

Ben appeared in the doorway. "What's up?" He didn't sound annoyed, which made Gabe feel better.

"We'd like to look at the wrecked footage," Tyler said. "The stuff with the glowing eyes."

George raised his eyebrows. "They're just animal eyes, little dudes, but you're welcome to see it. Come on in."

He grabbed a laptop from the dresser and sat on the end of the bed to pull up the footage. "I was doing some editing last night, trying to work around the shots. Though you know, I guess we could leave them in, now that I think of it. Like the three frogmen that the guy spotted were just returning to their brethren."

"That would be an interesting idea," Ben agreed.

He cued up the footage, and they all watched. The spot where the glowing eyes appeared was obvious as soon as the frogmen climbed over the railing. The eyes never moved, even when the triplets began splashing and wallowing through the edge of the water.

"You'd think all that noise would scare an animal off," Ben said.

"Maybe whatever it is sees people a lot," George said. "I've heard of bears that get so used to people that you can walk right up and feed them."

"Until they bite your head off," Ben said.

"You don't think that's a bear, do you?" Tyler's voice squeaked slightly, but everyone ignored him.

"Can we get a copy of this tape for Sean to look at? He's really good at video analysis. He might be able to tell what kind of animal it is."

George shrugged. "Fine with me. Just promise that if it is a bear, you don't tell the girls. I still need to shoot in that area. We didn't get anything useful tonight and Amy freaks out easily."

Gabe didn't like promising that, but he definitely wanted a copy of the footage. Especially since the eyes in the tape definitely looked like the ones in the video Sean had showed them. Was the Loveland Frog still around after all?

chapter 7

CASHING IN
ON FROGS

Sean was still hunched over his computer playing the video over and over when Gabe and Tyler finally crawled into bed. They woke to the sound of Ben pounding on the door. When Gabe crawled out of the bed and opened the door, his brother looked way too cheerful.

"Get dressed," he said. "We're going to talk to a local expert on the Loveland Frog!"

"There's a local expert?" Gabe said.

"That's what the guy tells me," Ben said. "I got an e-mail from him last night. So get dressed and grab a camera."

"Food!" Tyler moaned, peeking out from under the covers.

"We'll get breakfast on the way." Ben clapped

his hands. "Come on. Let's get going."

When his stomach was full and he was finally fully awake, Gabe wondered about the change in plans for the day. "I thought we would stick with George and his group."

"They're probably all still in bed," Ben said. "As I remember, George doesn't believe in getting up before noon."

They pulled up in front of a worn old Victorian house with peeling paint and floor boards missing from the front porch. "Now that looks like a movie set," Tyler said. "For a movie I don't want to be in."

"Your fear may be reasonable," Sean said. "I believe this building is in violation of several local building codes."

"I'm not scared," Tyler grumbled. "Just a little creeped out."

Gabe didn't say anything. He just gathered the small camera and hustled out of the van.

At least this should make for some interesting footage.

After carefully climbing the cracked and squeaking porch steps, Gabe stopped and stared at a hand-lettered cardboard sign tacked up next to the front door: "Loveland Frog Museum. Ring Doorbell for Admittance."

He looked back at his brother. "This is a museum?"

"That's what the website says." Ben pushed the doorbell, and they could hear the faint sound of croaking coming from inside.

They heard an odd scuffling from the other side of the door, and then the door cracked open and a pale blue eye in a wrinkled face peeked out at them. "Yeah?" a rough voice said.

"Dr. Soll?" Ben said. "I talked to you earlier about some information on the Loveland Frog for our Internet show *Discover Cryptids*."

The eye continued to look at them suspiciously. Then the voice snapped, "Show me your hands. All of you. The last kids at my door threw eggs at me."

Everyone held out both hands, though Tyler had to set down an equipment bag to do it. Finally the door opened.

The man on the other side had snow white hair that stuck out wildly from his head as if he ran his fingers through it often. He was barely taller than Gabe, and wore a bright blue shirt covered in big-eyed frog faces. "Welcome to the Loveland Frog Museum. Admittance is five dollars. Each."

"And what do we get for our money?" Tyler asked.

The man dropped his voice to a rough whisper. "The most complete collection of Loveland Frog artifacts in the world."

"I wasn't aware there were any Loveland Frog artifacts," Sean said.

"I'm very quiet about them," the man said.

Ben handed over a twenty-dollar bill. "Dr. Soll, you said on the phone that you'd seen the frog yourself?"

The old man examined the twenty carefully, not even looking up as he muttered, "Many times." Finally, he shoved the bill into his jeans pocket and waved them in. "Come on in. Since you're wanting an interview, you can come to my private office. I'll make everyone some tea. Only two dollars. Each."

"I'm not fond of tea," Sean said.

The old man glared at him. "You boys planning to be difficult?"

"They aren't," Ben insisted. "Tea would be lovely." He pulled a ten out of his wallet, and the old man snatched it out of his hand. No change was offered, but Dr. Soll spun on his heel and led them deeper into the house.

Now that they were inside, Gabe turned on the small camera and looked around. Every surface and every wall featured frogs. There were framed photos of frogs, and small frog sculptures. There were rough drawings of frogmen, also framed, and Gabe saw a television running the same video they had watched on Sean's laptop. The video played over and over on a loop.

Gabe paused by a table where a small spotlight shone on a stick. "Why do you have a light on a stick?"

"That's the stick that the frogmen shot sparks from in 1955. You can hold it if you want." Gabe started to reach for the stick, and the old man added, "Just four dollars."

Gabe shoved his hands into his pockets instead. "I'm good."

When they reached the "office," which Gabe

56

suspected had once been a dining room, he saw that every surface was piled with papers. He leaned over to look at some of the papers. They were printouts from web forums and comment streams on cryptid websites. He even recognized some of the URLs from research Sean had showed him.

The old man waved at some worn, straight-backed chairs that looked like they'd come from an old dining set. They all sat while Dr. Soll fussed with a battered kettle that sat on a single electric burner.

"Dr. Soll," Gabe said politely. "Have you ever heard of a curse associated with the Loveland Frog?"

The man squinted at him. "A curse?" He shook his head. "The frogmen are here to study us. In their own world, they are scientists."

"Their world?" Sean asked.

"Of course." Dr. Soll laughed, a wheezy

sound. "You see any frog people hanging around your town? They aren't from this world. Any numskull could see that."

Gabe sighed. They wouldn't be using any footage from this chat. The one thing Ben absolutely didn't ever have on the show was alien talk. Ben believed some cryptids were simply undiscovered species, while others were more like folktales with no real creature behind them.

"We met a man out near the river," Gabe said. "He told us there was a curse."

The transformation on the old man's face was startling. He looked furious. "Norton Wisk is a liar. He's always been a liar, and he'll always be a liar. If you bunch are working with him, you can get out right now."

"Sir," Ben said.

"Get out!" the old man screamed, his face turning red as he waved his arms. "Get out!"

chapter 8

HOP TO IT

"I'm getting tired of being yelled at by strangers," Tyler said when they reached the van.

"On the up side," Gabe said as he slipped into the seat behind Tyler. "We now know the name of the first guy who yelled at us."

Ben started up the van. "What we need is someone who can tell us about both these guys. And I think I know who."

Ben drove directly to a small brick building that housed a bakery on the bottom floor. "Your source is a baker?" Gabe asked.

"Nope." Ben pulling into one of the parking spaces at the front. "My source is above the bakery." They all hopped out of the van.

While Ben fed a parking meter, Gabe walked to the narrow door that lead upstairs. The sign on the door was nearly as crude as the one on the Loveland Frog Museum, but at least the lettering was done in paint on wood. It read, "Hop to It."

"What is that?" Gabe asked as he turned back to his brother.

Ben walked over and opened the door. "A weekly shopper. They mostly run business profiles, but I happen to know the editor, from some cryptid discussion boards. She has an interest in the frogman stories, so she should be able to tell us about Dr. Soll and Norton Wisk."

As it turned out, Ben was right. Bella Bleu was a thin woman in thick glasses who looked to be about Ben's age. "I love *Discover Cryptids*," she said when she shook Ben's hand. "How can I help your team?"

"Information." Ben explained about his

meeting with Dr. Soll and the man's odd reaction to the story of the curse.

"Oh, those two." Bella looked at Gabe who had his camera out to add footage for the show. She winced. "I'll tell you what I know, but not for the show."

Ben waved Gabe to put down the camera. "No problem."

"Soll and Wisk originally opened that strange museum together. But they had some kind of falling out. No one knows what exactly. I think it probably had something to do with money."

Tyler spoke up, "Dr. Soll certainly seems focused on money."

"Wisk too, so I expect they each wanted a bigger section of the deal. Wisk has been trying to drum up interest in frogman tours where he leads people around in the dark near the river. On one tour, he accidentally walked two of the customers right off the riverbank."

"He certainly didn't seem to want the movie crew around the wetlands near the river's edge," Ben said.

"He made a curse," Sean added.

Bella frowned. "It's odd that he wouldn't want the movie crew around. That sounds like exactly the kind of publicity that would help him sell his tour idea."

"Maybe he actually believes in the curse," Gabe suggested.

Bella laughed. "I doubt it." Since she had nothing new to offer about the two men, Bella let Gabe bring the camera back out. She showed them her own research on the Loveland Frog. "I even write about it in my newspaper sometimes. Everyone enjoys reading about the frog."

"What do you think of the video and still photos from 2016?" Sean asked.

"I'm not sure," she said. "Maybe the kids saw something, but I'm not sure it's real." A smile was playing at the corners of her mouth. "Did you look at the pictures closely?"

Sean nodded. "I could imagine several ways to produce the footage without any actual frogmen."

"So could I," Bella said. "Which doesn't mean I'm right. But I have my doubts."

Sean seemed very happy to chat with another skeptic, and Ben eventually had to practically drag him out.

"Where to now?" Gabe asked.

"Now we check out the area where George was filming last night," Ben said. "I want to see it in the daylight. Clearly Norton Wisk doesn't want anyone around there. I'd like to know why."

In the daylight, the swampy area near the road wasn't spooky at all. Ben pulled the van off the road and they all stepped over the guardrail to head into the brush. Gabe carried the small camera, so after he'd walked a few steps, he turned to film the guardrail from the swamp side. He thought it might be an interesting angle.

When he swept the camera view across the area, he saw something odd in the viewfinder. He walked back closer to the guardrail and knelt in the brush. Green bits of rubber lay half hidden in a clump of grass. Gabe picked up a piece. He recognized that color. They were rubber scraps from Meg's flipper. He held a scrap close to his nose, looking at the edges.

"What are you doing?"

Tyler's voice made Gabe jump. He hadn't heard his friend coming back through the brush. "Don't sneak up on me," he gasped.

"I wasn't sneaking," Tyler insisted.

Gabe held out a handful of rubber scraps. "I found the pieces from Meg's flipper."

Tyler shrugged. "I guess the rat decided it didn't like the taste after all."

"I don't think it was chewed," Gabe said. "The flipper looked chewed when I looked at it in the dark, but the edges of these pieces look cut. Someone cut a hole in the flipper."

"Why would someone do that?"

"To stop the filming or maybe to make the movie look cursed." Gabe shoved the scraps in his pocket. He looked out into the brush. "The big question is, how far will they go to stop the movie? Are George and his sisters in danger?"

"I have an even bigger question," Tyler said nervously. "Are we?"

chapter 9

SURPRISE SABOTEUR

The search of the swampy area turned up nothing else interesting. Ben announced they might as well grab some lunch before tracking down George.

During lunch, Ben's phone rang. He pulled it out of his pocket and put the call on speaker. "Hey, George!"

"My brother is still asleep," Jo's voice complained. "But we're starving."

"We're finishing up now," Ben said. "But we'll grab some food to go and bring it to you. Are burgers and fries okay?"

"Are you kidding?" Jo said. "We're ready to eat burgers and flies."

When they got back to the hotel, Ben sent

Gabe to take the girls a bag of burgers. Meg opened their room door, and snatched the bag out of Gabe's hand. Then the door closed. Gabe blinked at the closed door. "Um, you're welcome!" he shouted.

The door opened again. Jo reached out, grabbed Gabe's arm, and dragged him in. Then the door closed again. "Thanks," Jo said around a mouthful of burger. She sat on the edge of the bed next to her sisters. Gabe perched on the one room chair.

"What have you guys been doing?" Jo asked.

"Investigation and research." Gabe reached into his pocket and held out the scraps of rubber. "We went back to the bridge. I think someone cut a hole in Meg's flipper."

"The old guy?" Jo asked. "How would he get close enough without being seen?"

"I don't know, but I think he might be involved. He's been trying to get a business started doing tours around there, looking for the Loveland Frog."

Jo took another bite of burger. She chewed for a moment, then said, "That doesn't make sense. He should want the movie. It'll help make more people interested in the frog."

"That's what we thought," Gabe said. "A fake curse doesn't make sense."

Amy looked at him, her eyes wide. "It might not be fake."

Ignoring her sister, Jo said, "Maybe he wasn't trying to stop the movie. Maybe he just didn't want the movie to be right there."

Gabe shook his head. "We thought of that. It's one of the reasons we went back there today. Other than those scraps of rubber. We didn't find anything weird."

"That doesn't mean there wasn't something last night." Jo shoved the rest of the burger in her mouth and smiled as she chewed.

Just as she swallowed the big bite of burger, they heard a loud pounding on the door. When Jo answered, George burst in, holding up a large battery. "Someone swapped out the battery packs on the cameras with dead ones," he yelled. "That's why they stopped working." He pointed at the three girls. "A tech saw a frog near the equipment. So which of you did it?"

Gabe froze as the girls looked at one another. Then Amy burst into tears. "I just wanted to go home."

"What?" Jo and Meg said together.

Amy sniffled. "I'm tired of being hot and dirty and eating out of vending machines. I want to go home. I thought if everyone believed in the curse, we could go home."

Meg glared at her sister. "You ruined my favorite socks with swamp muck."

"I didn't mean to wreck your socks," Amy said. "It's not always about you, Meg."

Her sister just rolled her eyes.

"How did you get Norton Wisk to tell us that ridiculous curse story?" George asked.

"I didn't," Amy said in a tiny voice. "That's one more reason I want to go home. I don't want to be cursed."

George sighed. He turned to Gabe. "My sisters and I need a long talk. Do you mind if we have some family time?"

"No problem."

As Gabe headed out the door, George called

out, "Tell Ben we won't be filming tonight. I don't know about tomorrow."

"No more," Amy wailed.

"We'll see," George answered grimly. Then he flapped a hand at Gabe. "Go on. Tell Ben."

Gabe nodded and left. His brother was not going to like this.

chapter 10

WIDE-MOUTHED
HOAX

After pulling the van off the road, Ben turned in his seat to look at Gabe. "I don't see any value in coming back here. We know the stuff that happened last night wasn't anything to do with Norton Wisk."

Gabe scooted forward in his seat. "But we don't know why he invented a curse in the first place. Something is going on here, and it's tied to the Loveland Frog."

"Also," Sean added. "Your new focus on how cryptid stories influence human behavior ties directly to this. It appears both Dr. Soll and Norton Wisk seem to be trying to profit from the legends."

"If they are just legends," Tyler added. "Cause

that video online was creepy and so were those big eyes in George's movie footage. Something is out there."

Ben sighed. "Fine. Grab the night vision cameras and let's take a walk."

They didn't have to tramp far from the road before they heard Norton Wisk's voice, talking about the Loveland Frog. They pushed through the brush near the river and found the old man leading a group of people beside the river. Wisk turned to glare at them. "What are you doing here? You didn't buy a ticket for this tour!"

"We're filming for *Discover Cryptids*," Ben said. Gabe could tell he was using his show voice, so he quickly began filming. Ben turned to the group. "Has he told you about the Loveland Frog curse yet?"

"Curse?" a young woman said, her voice shaking. She turned to the man beside her. "You didn't say anything about a curse!"

"No one told me," the man said, turning an angry scowl toward Wisk.

"I didn't sign up to get cursed!" another man shouted.

"Look, it's nothing to worry about," Wisk said, smiling widely at the group. "These kids are just playing a prank. I promise, you're perfectly safe."

"He told us the Loveland Frog curses anyone who comes on this land," Tyler shouted.

The whole group took a step back away from Wisk.

"Why didn't you tell us about the curse?" the young woman asked. She sounded near tears. Then her wide eyes opened even wider. She pointed toward the river and screamed.

Everyone turned to look toward the water. Through the viewfinder, Gabe could clearly see someone slogging through the shallows of the river not far from the bank. From the big head, Gabe knew it had to be a frogman, or someone pretending to be a frogman. Gabe was impressed the person could keep his footing in the fast-moving water.

The screamer pushed through the rest of the group and ran for the road. That startled the rest of the tour group out of staring toward the water. They raced after her.

"Wait!" Wisk yelled. "Wait! It's perfectly safe.

The frogmen are our friends."

"Where did the frogman go?" Tyler asked.

Gabe had swung the camera toward Wisk when he was bellowing. Now he turned it back to the river. He swept it back and forth but he couldn't find the frogman.

"Maybe he went under," Tyler said.

"If he did, he would be swept downstream," Sean said.

Gabe figured that was right. He'd fallen in a river once and been swept away.

"I don't have to listen to you people," Wisk said. He turned to stomp away in the opposite direction of the road.

Ben crossed the clearing, reaching out for the man. "Hold on."

Wisk just picked up speed and pushed aside some brush. That's when Dr. Soll practically fell into the clearing. The old man struggled to catch his balance, but it was hard because he wore big frog flippers. He also had some kind of helmet on his head with two small flashlights taped to either side.

Gabe suspected the flashlights made big glowing frog eyes in the dark.

"There's your frogman," Tyler said.

"Fake!" Wisk yelled. "He's trying to ruin my tours."

Dr. Soll stomped closer and poked Wisk in the chest. "Don't think you're going to dump this all on me."

After some yelling and pushing, Wisk admitted he had come up with the idea of the Loveland Frog Dark Night tours and talked Dr. Soll into helping. "Everyone loves to be a little scared," Wisk said. "So, I suggested the tours."

"But why pretend you hated him?" Gabe asked Dr. Soll.

"I hated the lying. That's not what the museum is supposed to be about." He sighed loudly. "People weren't coming to the museum. I needed the money, but I didn't want anyone to think I liked this tour idea."

"You know," Tyler said. "Everyone knows scary movies and haunted house tours aren't real. They're safe scares. If you were honest with them, your tour group probably wouldn't have run away."

"And if you don't come clean," Ben said. "We're going to have to turn you in to the police."

Dr. Soll and Wisk looked at Ben in shock. "You'd do that?" Dr. Soll asked.

"Yeah," Ben said. "We would."

"You should have stayed in the water," Wisk growled at Dr. Soll. "What are you doing out here?"

"What are you talking about? I came to tell you that I don't want to get in," Dr. Soll said, his voice fretful. "The river is running too fast from all the rain we've had lately. I could drown."

"What do you mean, you don't want to get in?" Wisk demanded. "We all saw you."

"I have a video," Gabe added.

Sean reached out and touched the old man's wet suit. "This is dry." He bent and shone a light on the man's feet. "There is no river mud on these flippers."

Tyler's voice sounded squeaky as he asked. "Then what was in the water?"

They all turned to look at the river, but no one had an answer.

Later in their hotel room, the team gathered around Sean's computer as he brought up the video that Gabe shot of the river. There was no doubt that something with a big head was wading through the water.

"Maybe Wisk and Soll aren't the only ones playing frogman," Ben suggested.

"Maybe," Gabe said quietly as Sean ran

through the footage again. But in his heart, he sure hoped not. "This is going to be a cool episode even without the movie."

Ben cleared his throat. "Actually, George wants to finish the movie. But he's sending Amy and Meg home. It turns out Jo wants to keep filming."

"But doesn't he need three frogmen?" Tyler asked.

"He said he'd filmed most of the scenes where they need three kids in the suits." Ben paused and cleared his throat again. "I suggested I might know some kids who could wear the suits for the last few scenes."

"I am not putting on a frog suit," Sean announced. "Never, ever, no way."

Ben looked at Gabe and Tyler with a big grin. "Good thing there are three of you."

Gabe and Tyler looked at one another and shrugged. Then they both said, "Ribbit!"